Carlisle Writers' Group

WRITE CHRISTMAS!

Keep Dreaming…

Compiled by Susan Cartwright-Smith
Additional editing by Neil Robinson & John Nevinson

Carlisle Writers meet the first and third Monday of each month. We welcome new members and enjoy taking our work out to community groups in the city.

Please check out the blog carlislewritersblogspot.com for other work and information about the group.

Foreword

Since 2015, members of Carlisle Writers' Group have provided Christmas stories for Radio Cumbria's afternoon programmes in December.

Presenter Caroline Robertson invited us to make those first recordings, and now that we return each winter, it feels like a tradition has been established. The warmth of Caroline's friendly programme was reflected in the way she made uneasy readers relax and record their stories; we have really enjoyed working with her.

After the initial broadcast, many of the stories in this book disappeared into the ether, and have never appeared in print until now. We hope you enjoy them!

John Nevinson
CWG chair 2014-2018

Contents

THE SACRIFICE

Susan Cartwright-Smith

The soft glow from the candle light was almost enough to chase away any night time fears. And why should there be any fear? Tonight of all nights? But tonight held the worst terror of all – and it was only a matter of hours away.

The house was settling down after the day's activity; boards creaked as the wood cooled and the wind howled down the chimney like the screech of a wild beast. The smell of an extinguished fire carried on the air, and a sudden chill gripped the room. A soft knock at the door alerted the occupants to their visitors. With silent looks to each other, they took their seat at the table, and the eldest female opened the door. In scurried muffled shapes, identity-less in layers of wrappings. Nevertheless, the woman glanced them over, making sure they crossed over the horseshoe on the floor. She leaned out over the threshold, to check for late comers, and felt the pull and lure of the snowy, sparkling night, a yearning and physical tug. She forced herself to return to the damp chill of the room. She shivered. And carried the cold back in with her.

"Are we all here?" asked one of the room's occupants. As various layers were removed from heads, each person scrutinised the other.

"None left without," answered another, gruffly. Satisfied nods and grunts. The two women palmed their swollen bellies nervously. They knew that they at least had some kind of safety. But still they were afraid.

When all were seated, teeth chattering with cold, or perhaps fear, one of the older men cleared his throat.

"So tonight, as we know, one of us is to make the sacrifice."

A full silence gripped the room. Eyes dropped to laps.

"It is the way. We are fewer in number, this year, but we are ready". He looked around. "We are ready?" It was posed as a question this time. A murmured acquiescence satisfied him.

Then one spoke up. "Why should we bother?"

All turned to look at him. "Our sacrifice is for nothing. We grow fewer and weaker, and yet more is asked of us, expected of us. Always more, and forgotten in an instant. What is the point?"

No-one spoke for some minutes. Then the original speaker continued. "It is our way and our custom. It is what we do. What we have always done, since the original records, what our kind is expected to do. Do you think you are outside of our law? Is this life not for you?"

"This is no life. Knowing your destiny is sacrifice."

The first man shook his heavy head, his shaggy locks and beard hiding his expression.

"I cannot answer that. It is for the fates to decide. If you do not wish to take part I cannot force you, but I don't expect you will be welcome at any house hereafter."

Another silence. The speaker turned slightly to one of the gravid female. "Shall we begin?"

She bustled in her terror, as she set bowls and spoons before all assembled. She stirred the swollen bellied pot, which held its warmth from the extinguished fire. The other woman assisted as they carried the pot to the table, and heaved it into place. Each bowl received a stirred helping of broth. The expectation held each diner in talons, as they lifted their spoons. The women held on to each other in premature grief. They were spared this ritual at least, but the anticipation was torturous. Still, they were involved in the sacrifice. Still they were complicit.

Each man had taken a spoonful, And another. Then a groan of – what, fear? Disappointment? It was hard to tell. Each head turned in the direction of the reaction. It was the Elder, the dried bean resting in his hand. He caught the eye of the dissenter.

"If I am to be the one, then it is right and proper and the fates have spoken. But you, you with your youth and strength, you must keep our ways. Can you promise me, before I go out to do what must be done? Promise me you will keep our ways alive?"

The younger man looked up with hurt in his eyes. "I can only try. I cannot promise. Just try."

The elder knew that this would have to suffice, but he felt a weariness descend upon him. He hung his head, seemingly aged in the last few minutes, his thick hair glinting in the candlelight.

"My family, it is our duty to continue this tradition," he began, "or perhaps," he laughed bitterly, "it is our curse."

He held his hand out to the older woman, who had served the broth. "Do not fret so. Your job is to carry on the line. After tonight I will not return. You know this. It is impossible to carry out this task and live. I will be thinking of you as I ride out. I carry in me the blood of our ancestors, the inheritance that makes this night possible."

He paused his conversation. The clock on the mantle ticked loudly. Then stopped.

"It is time. I must ready myself. Please bring the carriage round."

Two of the men left to the back of the house. The younger woman went to the cupboard and brought out the thick travelling cloak, which he shouldered in to, roughly. The elder woman brought a belt which she reached around him, her belly against his, her movements clumsy. He touched her face, lightly, his thumb brushing away a tear. He smiled at her, his eyes crinkling with a merriment he did not feel. She kissed the heel of his hand, and then stood away from him, smoothing her apron down.

The stamp of hooves and jingle of harness suggested the carriage was ready. He reached for the hat which hung by the door, on the stand, and put it on as he opened the door, letting in a gust of icy air. He looked out, taking in the scene – the snow just starting to fall, the hot breath of the beasts in harness smoking in the night. He climbed aboard, looking back to check his burdensome cargo was in place. Satisfied he was ready, he took up the reins and slapped them against waiting rumps.

The last vestiges of magic coursing through his veins tingled as he left the boundary of the village, left their enchantment, knowing that his sacrifice was expected, his torture would tear at him, seemingly forever, but his life would be over in the time it took for the tinkle of a Christmas bell to fade away. This was the curse of their bloodline.

"On Dasher, On Dancer!" he yelled, as he urged the reindeer on, up, up into his endless night.

A GIFT FOR CHRISTMAS

John Nevinson

Annie and Jack Graham would try as hard as they could to make it a decent Christmas for Sarah, but they both knew it would be a kind-hearted and loving gesture… and a futile one. Edward had gone away in mid-October, on the troop train out of the noise and smoke of the Citadel Station with his Border Regiment comrades; the official letter had come on a murky day in November to say that their son had not survived the muddy hell of the trenches near Ypres. And there was his young wife Sarah, a twenty year-old lass he'd only married last midsummer, left alone in the cottage at Torpenhow.

Jack and Annie were numbed by the loss of their boy, and terrified that their only other son Richard would also be taken from them; but they loved their red-headed daughter-in-law, and wanted to support and help her through the dark winter to come. Annie suggested only the once that Sarah move to stay with them at Wigton for a few weeks, to see her through the first bad days, but the girl held her hand and said, "Thanks, Mam. Whether I'm in your house or mine, our Eddie won't be there, will he? And somehow I think I need to be alone in my own place just now, and sort myself out in my own time…"

The older woman hugged her, and thought how she and Jack would be supporting each other, and how solitary Sarah would be at Rowan Tree Cottage with her thoughts. "And alone with her tears, I suppose", mused Annie, and she thought of animals who hid themselves away when they were ill, and who came out of their self-imposed exile when they had recovered.

"I understand, Sarah love," whispered Annie. "But there's one time you just cannot be alone, and that's Christmas."

"Oh, Mam, I couldn't face Christmas…"

"But Jack and me, we'll have to, my dear. And… and… Don't you think we will find it so hard without our boy? We will need you to help us."

Sarah felt a twinge of guilt. Yes, of course the couple missed Edward, in a painfully different way than her own, and she thought of his school photographs and the silver christening bowl on their oak sideboard. She sighed and shivered. "Yes, you are right. It's a time we shouldn't be separated. Yes, I will come over on Christmas morning."

As it turned out, Jack's cousin Rob, a widower from Cockermouth, was travelling into Carlisle to spend Christmas with his daughter's family, and he said he would pick up Sarah, and drop her off at Wigton. The only trouble was that Rob was going to Carlisle on Christmas Eve, as he loved to see his grandchildren open their presents before the family went to the service at the Cathedral, so it meant that Sarah would have to stay overnight with her in-laws, and he'd call in to take her home late on Christmas Day afternoon.

There was sleet in the air when the cart dropped the young widow at Blackmire Cottage, and after a few hugs, Rob went gratefully to a happy house in Carlisle, and felt relieved that he wasn't going to be with the sad trio. Sarah took her overnight things to the spare bedroom, the one that Eddie had shared with his brother Richie; in a way, it was easier to sleep there knowing it wasn't just Eddie's room, but she had to push away the unpleasant thoughts of nineteen year-old Richie, at this very moment wallowing in the slime of Passchaendale.

Sarah and Annie worked away all that evening in the stone-flagged kitchen, preparing the goose, potatoes and vegetables for the Christmas dinner. The women tired themselves out, and Jack drank a little more than usual, so that the three of them slept soundly in their beds.

The Wigton church bells woke Sarah on Christmas morning, and she lay in bed dreamily until she realised that her in-laws had been up and about for a while. By the time she went into the cosy living room, the warmth and smell from the kitchen hit her, and she felt momentarily queasy. "The windows are well steamed-up, my lass," beamed Jack, as Annie walked in rubbing her hands on her apron. "Eh, goose fat!" she smiled. "The bird's only been in for thirty minutes, and I'm already bailing out the roasting tin!" There was a quiet contemplative moment, and then the three of them hugged gently, murmuring a muted "Happy Christmas," and sat down to some breakfast.

Jack carved the big goose sometime after midday, and Annie got Sarah to help her sort out the roast potatoes, vegetables, gravy and trimmings. They ate with slightly theatrical bravura—it hid the fact there should have been five of them at the feast. At the end of the meal, which Jack had raced through, they sat back and felt guiltily full and satisfied.

Then Jack tottered to the sideboard and brought over three glasses and a bottle of port.

"A toast!" he mumbled, dropping back on to his chair.

"Not yet, Dad! We've still got the Christmas pudding..." began Annie.

"Oh, the pudding can wait, woman!" he cut in, waving away her plea dismissively.

For the first time, Sarah felt uncomfortable. Was her father-in-law going to raise some kind of maudlin toast, which would upset them all after the remarkable way they had held themselves together on this emotional day? She could see Annie seemed anxious, as she too wanted everything to stay calm and steady, and the two women locked their eyes on each other while Jack hauled himself to his feet.

"To... absent friends. Richie and... our Eddie!"

And at that strange moment, time seemed to slow down to a dreamlike speed. The light appeared more sharp and intense as Sarah looked at the oak sideboard with the photo of Eddie, his silver christening bowl and its Christmas card with the baby in the manger, and the young widow felt a mild sensation low in her stomach. She glanced at a smiling Annie, who seemed intuitively in harmony with her. Absent friend? Eddie? No, Eddie was here now... in this room... in her!

And in a wonderful miraculous way, the best Christmas gift she'd ever had, Sarah knew that her man would be alive again next summer.

A BABY CALLED HOUDINI

Len Docherty

Jack Mason, aged six, was looking forward to Christmas, even though it was only early November. He had posted his letter to Santa Claus, but didn't expect to receive very many of the toys on his list. Although still very young, Jack had a sensible head on his shoulders. Many of his school pals came from rich families, and could afford anything. Jack knew that his parents, Tom and Susan, never had much money to spend. His mum worked in a clothes shop in town, and was also a barmaid in the *Nag's Head,* three nights a week. His dad was a mechanic at a local garage, but wasn't well paid.

At school, Jack was always top of his class, and his pals were jealous. They used to boast about their posh houses and parents, but Jack never took the bait. He knew that money might be able to buy lots of things, but brains weren't one of them. He wanted to get a good education; a good job, and to be able to help his parents to enjoy a better life.

One day, Jack was walking home from school. His home was about a mile from school, and though he enjoyed the exercise, this day was hard work. It had snowed overnight, and started melting during the day. The slush was making walking hard work, while penetrating Jack's shoes. He knew that he needed new shoes, but he made do, as money was tight.

Meanwhile, in a land far away, an army of overworked elves were making Christmas presents for millions of children. Santa and Mrs Claus might bring happiness to youngsters, but to the elves, they were cruel slave drivers. Factory Claus was not a happy place of work, and hadn't been for some time. Originally, Santa had put the elves on zero hours, and this didn't go down well. The elves' leader, Elvis, told his workforce to down tools, until Santa saw sense. Santa dug his heels in, thinking it to be a storm in a teacup.

The elves however, were defiant, and Elvis informed Santa, that if he failed to deliver Christmas presents to the many needy children, his name would be mud. The stand-off, lasted for a further two weeks, but after another two incidents, Santa had to give in. Santa's sleigh shed a runner, and he thought he could just buy a replacement. On checking, Santa found that the supplier had been made insolvent, and he couldn't find a replacement supplier. If that wasn't bad enough, there was a problem with Rudolph's nose. Factory Claus hadn't entered the age of technology, and was still in abacus mode. The sleigh didn't possess a Sat-Nav, relying instead on Rudolph's red nose. Unfortunately, life's wear and tear had taken the reddish glow away, and he was unable to follow his nose! So to speak...

These happenings were doing nothing for Santa's blood pressure. It did however, mean that his cheeks were naturally red, and he wouldn't need to pinch the rouge from Mrs Claus this year. He had a meeting with Elvis, and agreed to put the elves on regular contracts until the New Year. The elves reluctantly returned to work, and Santa gave them overtime to help them catch up with the backlog. If Santa thought his troubles were over, he was wrong. Mrs Claus worked in the office, and like Santa, she was a 'technology virgin.' She didn't know her text from her twitter, and was getting behind with the paperwork for the Christmas presents. Santa's face was getting redder and redder, and he accused her of 'loitering within text.' She burst into tears, and he had to promise to take her on holiday, to placate her. He agreed that they would both gain from going to technology lessons, in the New Year. At last, everyone in Factory Claus was singing from the same song-sheet.

Meanwhile, back in the real world, Jack was slithering his way home, complete with soggy feet. He thought he heard someone cry out, and looking back, saw that an old man had slipped in the slush, and fallen over. Jack wasn't sure what to do, as his parents had told him to beware of strangers. He realised that the old man was in no position to harm him, and hurried over to him. He recognised him as Silas Brooks; said to be the local miser. Jack was caught in two minds: should he help this old miser, or walk by on the other side? Luckily, Jack had been brought up properly by his parents, and he asked the old man how he could help?

"I think I might have broken my leg, young man. Can you get an ambulance?"

"I think so," Jack answered. "I don't have a phone, but I'll run to the nearest house, and get them to phone. I'll be as fast as I can." He ran, or rather slithered through the slush, to a nearby house. He explained the position to the man who answered the door, and pointed to the old man.

"Come in and wait," the man said to Jack. "No, I have to get home; mum will worry if I'm late home." He slithered off, leaving the man open mouthed, but returned to the old man, and told him an ambulance would be there soon.

"Thank you, young man. What's your name?"

"Jack," he said. "I must get home. Hope you are soon better." He slithered off, not giving the old man a chance to say anything else.

When Jack arrived home, he was surprised to find his mum was already home from work. "Hi, mum, you're home early?"

"Yes, I wasn't feeling too well. Anything to tell me?"

"No, mum, just an ordinary school day. Do you need a hand with anything?"

"No, son, I'm just tired. I'll have a lie down, and then I'll make the tea." She disappeared upstairs, leaving Jack looking worried. When Jack's dad came home, mum was still upstairs.

"Dad, is there something wrong with mum, she isn't often ill?"

"It's nothing son, she just has an upset tummy. I'll go and check if she's going to get up for tea?"

Back at Factory Claus, it was a hive of industry. The elves were hard at work; sweating hard. They wouldn't need to go to weight watchers anytime soon. Santa's face had turned a lighter shade of red: worry lines had abated. Between them, he and the elves had managed to mend the runner, and had put it back on the sleigh. He *still* had the problem of Rudolph's nose to sort out. He went to the local electrical store, and explained his predicament to the manager. Minutes later, he left the store smiling, and holding a box containing a large red bulb. Arriving back at Factory Claus, he summoned Rudolph to the office. Rudolph came, and left with a large red bulb attached to his battered nose. A wire protruding from the bulb was attached to a switch attached to his neck. He was not happy: Oh dearie me! Mrs Claus had managed to get up to date with all her paperwork, and things were going well.

Meanwhile, Jack's mum had been off work for a few weeks, and Jack was fretting. He wondered what was wrong, as both mum and dad were being evasive. He'd always been told to be truthful, but he felt his parents weren't being. His schoolwork started to suffer, and it got worse when he was summoned to the headmaster's office. He was told by the headmaster, that a local man had been trying to trace him, as he'd recently helped him when he'd fallen. Jack was worried what his parents would say, but the head said the old man wanted to reward him.

At home, Jack's parents were pleased to hear about how he'd helped the old man. Jack felt relieved he wasn't in trouble, and took the opportunity to ask what was wrong with his mum. His parents both blushed, but eventually, told him that he would soon have a brother or sister. Jack didn't know how to react, but said he was pleased that mum wasn't going to die. His parents laughed, and Jack was happy again. What a Christmas present!

Next morning, a letter arrived. It was from Silas Brooks, and was an invite for Jack and his parents to spend Christmas at his mansion. They accepted.

Christmas Eve, and the sleigh was loaded up for its first trip. Rudolph, complete with his Red Nose Bulb set off. The journey was traumatic, as the sleigh struggled through thick clouds, which slowed it down. A number of times, Rudolph thought he was going to lose his Red Nose, but it stopped on, and the trip was successful.

Jack came down on Christmas morning, and there were no presents. He was crestfallen, but dad said they were at Silas Brook's mansion. They set off for the mansion; Jack not noticing his mum's absence.

Silas greeted them at the mansion door, and they were shown into the vast front parlour. There were mounds of presents, and sitting on the settee, was mum, and the new baby.

"What should we call him, Jack? As it's Christmas, we could call him Jesus?"

Jack blushed, and muttered something under his breath.

"What was that, Jack?" his dad asked.

"Well", Jack said, smiling," As he arrived here, down the chimney, without wrapping, and getting dirty, he should be called Houdini!"

Everyone laughed, and Silas wished everyone...

A Happy Christmas.

NATURE RESERVED

Jean Hill

A wild place lassoed by a track,
No geese calling:
Fresh logs in an orderly stack,
Rank cattle steaming;
Trees stretch bare and black
Creased pond gleaming;
I launch my foot, feel the ice crack
You save me from falling.

SNOWBELL

Alison Nixon

"Hark at her. Who does she think she is? Cinderella?" Silence.

"Cinderella, are you home?" The voice sang out again, this time with a coating of irritation.

Krystal could hear his voice, but couldn't see him. Trying hard she opened her eyes. *Oh wow*, it was magical. A blanket of white surrounded her. It was like Christmas. In the distance she could just make out the spires of a church, and loads of sparkly frosted trees. Home was in an orchard, knee deep in snow, at the bottom of a large farmhouse garden, and she was not alone.

"Well, you've found your eyes my dear, but not your manners I think."

Who was the rude speaker of that voice, she looked round to see the best she could. Well, she was a snowman, technically a snowwoman, and turning your head, speaking or blinking carried many risks: if something fell off, you were a bit stuck.

"Over here, Cinders."

Krystal stared into the morning gloom. There in the corner was a sorry mound of snow which moved slightly, shedding a skin.

The snowman had obviously seen better days, with large twigs for arms, what looked like a cock sided pirate hat on his head, a tatty Man Utd scarf round his neck, and, just like her, large lumps of coal for eyes, a stumpy carrot nose and his mouth was a simple plain hole. Large black buttons shone down his breast. His name, I will tell you, is Cyril, or the old git, as he is affectionately known in snowman circles.

"My name is Krystal." Krystal's voice surprised even her - it was the first time she'd used it and it was great. "My name is Krystal. My name is Krystal!" She repeated.

"We heard you the first time," Cyril grumped.

"My name is Krystal, and you are so rude. Snowmen are supposed to be kind and friendly." Krystal felt empowered.

"Cyril the snowman has rude running through him like in Blackpool rock, ha ha! He can't help himself!" This was another voice, and Krystal looked to see where it was coming from. He was just beside her, and *OMG he was so handsome*, she could melt. He too had big coal eyes, a carrot nose, and he was dressed in a red silk shirt, or rather, it was somewhat flung over his shoulders. He was positively the most handsome thing on ice.

"I'm Krystal," she blushed.

"So you said. Never mind old grumpy socks over there. He's half melted and water sodden. Took a bad hit yesterday morning before the weather turned and the snow came back, and they rolled you. I'm glad they did, you're so much prettier to look at. I'd shake your hand, but, you know I'll snap my twig, ha ha. I'm Sebastian. Seb will do."

"*I'm pretty?*" Krystal looked down; she had no buttons or a shirt, nor a hat. But oh my, she was naked as the day she was rolled.

"I'm humming your name, because it's such a great name to hum. Oh, who's she then?"

The ginger cat stopped in front of Krystal, sitting down.

"That cat can talk!" she exclaimed to Seb.

"It's not every day you hear a talking snowman either you know!"

The ginger cat was at her feet looking up, eying a good landing spot. Shoulder or head?

"Don't even think about it fur ball," Seb warned.

He rubbed himself around her, purring, before spotting Cyril.

"My Cyril, you're wasting away."

"Morning Ginger," he growled. "Goodbye."

"Who's the new girl?" He gestured to Krystal.

"How should I know? She appeared yesterday afternoon."

The ginger cat rubbed himself against him, making Cyril sneeze,

"Get lost puss, I'm *alergictic* to cats." He sneezed again showering the ginger tom in ice.

"You'll miss me when you're gone." He stopped to scratch his ear. "It's to turn mild tomorrow, too bad," he mumbled under his breath.

"I heard that. *Eyes front, Ginger.* Turn that business end away from me. No spraying!"

Ginger sat purring, staring at Cyril, tail twitching, before suddenly taking a leap at his pirate hat. Ginger, the hat and sadly Cyril's head disappeared in a cloud of snow underneath the hedge.

"Emily, how much stuff have you got on this sledge?" Tom was pulling it through the snow. They were going down to the orchard to build more snowmen, and sledge.

Emily, and their cousin Erin, were bringing up the rear; they had got all of two foot. The snow was unbelievably deep and stubborn. *Or it might be the sly fact that they were girls*, a fact Tom didn't feel confident to share as two versus one in a snowball fight would not end well.

"We're gonna dress the snow girl we built yesterday."

"Then we're gonna sledge."

"Yeah."

"Look that snowman's lost his head!" Erin pointed at Cyril.

"Where's his Man United scarf?" Tom was aghast. "Never mind we'll rebuild him."

"Look Erin, this is my snowman," Emily said proudly. "She's gonna be - a princess, a snowbell, gorgeous like Aunty Lindy. Daddy said so and that she was his snowbell when he came home on Saturday night when she babysat us."

"No, he didn't, Emily," Tom scolded his little sister; she was such a tale teller. "Mum and Dad were at Mark and Elaine's Christmas party."

"He did too, Tom. I was awake and going for some milk. I got to the stairs and he came home. I saw them. He said next time he kisses her like that it will be under the mistletoe. But Mummy's still his favourite snowbell. I'll ask her later when she's home from work."

"What are you doing with all these clothes, Emily? Isn't that mummy's favourite blouse?" Tom held up a light green print shirt.

"She's got to be pretty and smart Tom. Mint."

"I really don't think lipstick will stick to snow Emily." Erin tried to smear it on Krystal's lips, but the snow just fell off.

"See, Erin, I made some cut out lips and eyelashes."

An hour later they were done. Krystal, dressed in a green blouse, silk scarf, woolly pink hat, and rain coat to keep out the chill, the children, satisfied, set off up the hill to enjoy their sledging.

"They forgot about you, Sebastian." Krystal sounded upset.

"Thank God. Poor Cyril, they put his new head on back to front!"

Next day was mild and stormy; the children were heartbroken - their snowmen began to melt. Once the rain stopped they headed to the orchard with mummy.

"They're dead mummy, they're dead! My princess is gone!" Emily was hysterical.

"Sweetheart, they've simply melted, she's here in this puddle, see this is her heart full of love and cuddles". Mummy scooped some of the melted snow in to a small container. "We'll put it in the freezer and when it's cold enough and the snow comes again, we'll bring her out and roll her back to life."

"She'll be a princess again, Mummy. She'll be my very own princess. A snowbell, just like Aunty Lindy is Daddy's snowbell. He must think so an awful lot if he's gonna kiss her again but under the mistletoe!"

STORM SANTA

Len Docherty

After storm Desmond, families were looking forward to Christmas. The Thompson family had just missed being flooded, and were relieved, as they had been flooded in 2005.

Christmas morning dawns for the Thompson family: the sound of happy children, Jason 6, and Sophie 4, have been awake for hours, and they rush for their parcels, excitement oozing from every pore. Parents, Jill and Peter entered the front room: two weary souls, looking in need of sleep.

"Happy Christmas, Mummy and Daddy!" the children yelled as one.

"Happy Christmas, both!" the parents replied. "Hope Santa has brought you everything you asked for. Don't know how he manages to get everything on his sleigh, or how long it must take him to get it all delivered!"

"We saw him, didn't we Sophie?" Jason told them.

"Yes", Sophie replied, laughing, "And he was in a boat."

"Of course he was", Peter said, "you'll be telling us that he was rowing the boat."

"Yes, he was, how did you know that Daddy, did you see him as well?"

"No, he didn't," Jill said, blushing, "and neither did you two, you must have been dreaming."

"Yes," Peter said drily, "if you were grown- ups, I'd tell you to put more water in your whisky!"

"We weren't dreaming - Santa was wearing a red diving suit, and goggles, and Mrs Claus had a life- jacket over her coat," Jason insisted. "And the Reindeer all had life-jackets on."

Back in Lapland, Santa, Mrs Claus, and the reindeer were slumped, exhausted after the night of all nights.

"I'm ashamed of you all," Mrs Claus retorted. "I told you to dim the lights on the boat, but as usual, Santa, you knew best. I'm sure I saw a couple of children looking out of window at us. I bet they thought it was a spaceship!"

"You've got a cheek," Santa wearily replied. "I had everything to organise; had to help load the boat, and steer in the murk as well."

"You didn't steer the boat," Mrs Claus said, tugging his beard angrily. "All you did was hurl the presents down the chimneys."

"Yes," shouted Rudolph and the other reindeer, "and you missed quite a few."

"It wasn't as easy as you lot make out: some houses don't have chimney pots, and where there are flats, I have to enter by magic."

"Magic, my foot", they all chorused. "We've never seen so many broken windows!"

"I'm not listening to another word. I'm off to bed: waken me in July. No, make it August!" Santa left the room; muttering 'Bah! Humbug!' to himself.

"I'm worried about him," Mrs Claus said to the reindeer. "What will we do next Christmas, if he doesn't make it? There's only One Santa Claus."

"Well, Mrs Claus." Rudolph said, laughing. "You could colour your beard white and take his place!" All of the reindeer roared with laughter, tears running down their faces.

"Listen, you four-legged no-hopers. If Santa doesn't make it, you'll all finish up as venison burgers!" She laughed a wicked laugh, and The reindeer *stopped* laughing. "Now, it's sleeping time. See you in July; in the flesh, or a burger." She left the room, still laughing a wicked laugh.

"I wonder what a venison burger tastes like?" Rudolph said.

"There's only way to find out," Prancer and Dancer chorused as one.

"How?" Rudolph queried.

"By becoming the world's first cannibal reindeer!" The other reindeer laughed.

Meanwhile, back at the Thompson house, Jason and Sophie had opened all their presents, and couldn't believe their luck. Jason had lots of Lego, and a Star Wars Suit: Sophie, a Dolls House, and lots of clothes. Peter was reading a book the children had bought him, Jill was slaving in the kitchen.

"I'm hungry, Mum. When will we be eating?" Jason shouted.

"In about 10 minutes. Is that okay?" she shouted back.

"I suppose," Jason replied. He sat down on the floor and started to read his new Christmas book.

Peter put his book down and joined the children on the floor. "What did Santa leave you this year, kids?"

"Well, Daddy, I got a Tiffany Doll, a *Frozen* Magical Story Cape, a Disney Princess Royal Kitchen and Café, and a *Frozen* DVD."

"What about you, Jason?"

"Lots of stuff, Daddy, a remote BMW Controlled Car, a Pool Table, a BMX Bike, and a *Spiderman* DVD."

"Can we watch *Frozen*, Daddy?" Sophie asked

"No, we're going to watch *Spiderman*, aren't we Daddy?"

"No," came Jill's voice from the kitchen. "The meal's ready, can you all sit at the table. Peter, can you come and carve the turkey, please?"

Later...

"Do you all want Brussels,and turnip?"

"Yuk," replied both Jason and Sophie, "they smell awful, but we'll have peas, please."

The meal progressed...

"Mummy and Daddy, I know you don't believe us, but we really did see Santa and his helpers in a boat didn't we, Sophie?" Jason persisted.

"Yes, and they were wearing life jackets to keep them from drowning," Sophie commented.

"Mrs Claus was rowing the boat, and Santa was delivering the presents."

"What were the reindeer doing?" Peter persisted.

"The breaststroke," Jason said, and Jill and Peter laughed out loud.

"Just eat up," Jill told the children.

"It's not fair, you won't believe me and Sophie," Jason said.

"OK, we do believe you, but you must admit it conjures up a strange picture?"

"What does *conjures up* mean?" Sophie wanted to know.

"It means magic," Peter said, "but then, Christmas *is* magic."

"As the weather has been stormy, we should give Santa a new title, just for this year. What do you think, kids?"

"I guess," Jason and Sophie replied, "but what could we call him?"

"Well," said Jill, "we've had Storm Desmond, how about Storm Santa?"

"Yes, Mummy that's brilliant!" the children yelled. "We didn't know you were so clever!"

"Mummy doesn't just sit here all the time and do nothing", Peter said, smiling. "Well, not *all* the time, anyway"

Jill playfully slapped Peter, and all was well with the world.

CHRISTMAS PRESENTS

Neil Robinson

Caroline was surprised when her husband returned home in high spirits. Christmas Eve services invariably got him down. The church was always full, and although that might seem to be a cause for rejoicing, Nicholas knew he wouldn't see most of those in attendance for another twelve months. Of course, he took the opportunity to preach a suitably challenging sermon, but it never resulted in greater numbers during the year. Tonight, though, he was whistling when he came in - *It Came Upon A Midnight Clear* - and pulled off his dog collar with a flourish.

'Well,' Caroline said, 'somebody's full of Christmas cheer'.

'Yes, I am,' he beamed. 'You'll never guess who turned up at the service tonight.'

Caroline smiled. 'You're right. I won't,' she said.

'Old whatsisname. After all this time. Haven't seen him for years and I look down at all those candle-lit faces and there he is, hardly a day older than when we saw him last.'

'You're going to have give me more than that,' Caroline said. 'Which whatsisname is this?'

'You know, Matthew Storey, from the time we were in Birmingham. What a tonic he was - still is. He waited till all the mince-pie eaters had gone and we sat down at the back of the church with a cup of mulled wine and had a good old chin wag.'

'Not too much mulled wine, I hope,' Caroline said. Nicholas ignored her chiding.

'Fairly cheered me up,' he continued. 'Told me how much I'd helped him all those years ago and how he'd always meant to thank me. As he was passing he thought now was the perfect time.'

'That was kind of him,' Caroline said. It pleased her that this old friend had given her husband some much needed encouragement. 'You should've brought him back. I'd have liked to have seen him.'

'Oh, I told him that, but he said he needed to hit the road again for tomorrow's big day. Still, I'm glad he called in. Very glad.'

'That's good, dear. You and he should keep in touch,' but with Nicholas lost in reverie, she reached down and switched off the tree lights. 'Time to call it a day,' she said. 'The girls will be here before we know it.'

'Yes, you're right,' her husband said absently. 'I'll be up shortly.'

He sat at the fire after she'd gone and raked over its dying embers. 'Matthew Storey,' he said. 'Fancy. After all these years.'

He must have dozed off, because he awoke with a jolt when Caroline cried out from the bedroom. 'Nick!' she called, 'Nick! Come here, quickly!' She was sitting bolt upright in bed, the local paper spread out on the duvet in front of her. 'Matthew Storey was in church tonight, was he?' she said, with what Nicholas thought was irritation.

'You know he was. I just told you.'

'Well, look', she said, jabbing at the paper, 'Look!'

'What am I looking at?' he said, bewildered.

She picked up the paper again. 'Here', she said impatiently. 'Here!' and she read: "Police are appealing for witnesses to a fatal crash on the A56 on Wednesday 23rd December," - '23rd December', Caroline repeated emphatically, 'that's yesterday, Nick'. - "A police spokesman said road conditions were particularly treacherous and that the collision resulted in the death of West Midlands man, Matthew Storey, aged 56."

'Yes,' Nicholas nodded, 'That's what I said: Matthew was passing so he called in, one last time.'

BARNABY AND BERNADETTE

Pat Harkness

'Twas the night before Christmas

And all through the house

Not a creature was stirring

Not even a mouse...

except that is in a tiny cottage in Cumbria where there lived a family of mice. Mum and Dad and their two children, Barnaby and Bernadette, shared their home with a human family, and they were all looking forward to Christmas. Christmas meant more food, more cheese, more chocolate and lots of presents!

When the Christmas tree arrived Bernadette had spent all her spare time sitting at the mouse hole gazing longingly at the tree and sighing deeply. When Barnaby asked her what it was that attracted her so she said, "I just love looking at the tinsel and the baubles, but most of all, the fairy on the top. Do you see the dress she is wearing Barnaby, all shimmery and sparkly, with wings like gossamer? Oh, how I wish I could have a dress like that to wear on Christmas Day, but I don't suppose I will," she said sadly.

Now Barnaby was a kind hearted little mouse so he decided to climb to the top of the tree and get the dress for his sister. There was just one thing in his way. The human family had brought home a cat, yes, a large evil looking tom called Mr T and as everyone knows cats just love to chase mice! Night after night Barnaby had tried to reach the tree, but each time Mr T had spotted him and chased him back to the mouse hole. It could be very dangerous being a mouse!

Christmas Eve arrived, and it was Barnaby's last chance. He decided to wait until it was very late and everyone was fast asleep, especially Mr T. Barnaby was really tired but when he had heard Bernadette whisper "I wish I had a dress like the fairy," he was determined to stay awake.

The cottage was still and silent in the dead of night and it was very dark as Barnaby sneaked out of the mouse hole. He could just make out the shape of the Christmas tree by the light of the moon. It was now or never! Slowly he tiptoed across the floor and clambered up on to a chair. The tree looked as high as a mountain - could he really climb that high? Yes, he decided he could, anything for Bernadette. Slowly and very carefully he climbed up through the branches, taking great care not to disturb the decorations on the tree, but just as he got to the top to reach out for the dress, his tail caught one of the baubles and it fell. The noise it made as it hit the floor sounded deafening.

Barnaby hid inside the branches quaking with fear. Sure enough, the noise had disturbed the cat and it was now creeping towards the tree. Barnaby trembled as the cat looked up and spotted him. But instead of climbing up the tree the wily cat lay down right in front of the mouse hole. Poor Barnaby was trapped! Mr T glared up at him and licked his lips in anticipation of a juicy little mouse, a tasty treat for Christmas.

They heard a creaking noise on the roof followed by soft footsteps – and then the door slowly opened. Barnaby glimpsed something black, then red then white, and shrank back into the tree. It had looked like a giant! Then a kindly voice said "Well now, what do we have here?" Mr T ran and hid in the corner, but Barnaby peeked out to have a look. Imagine his surprise when the giant turned out to be none other than Santa Claus! Why nobody was frightened of Santa, except it seemed a scaredy cat called Mr T!

"What are you doing up there little mouse?" the kind old gentleman asked.

"P - please, sir," said Barnaby, still trembling. "I'm Barnaby," and then proceeded to tell Santa his story.

"Well, that was very brave of you," said Santa. "Perhaps I can help?"

"Oh, thank you sir," said Barnaby, "but you see the dress is far too big for my sister so it's hopeless, I'm afraid," and with that two large tears ran down Barnaby's cheeks.

"Now, now," said Santa, "we can't have this, not on Christmas Eve! Dry your eyes, Barnaby, and I will tell you what we will do. I will help you back to your mouse hole and then - well, just you leave the rest to me!"

"Oh, thank you, Santa," he sniffed. "It *is* way past my bedtime, but what about Mr T?" He pointed to the still cowering cat.

"Oh, don't worry about him," said Santa. "Everybody should be asleep when I bring them presents and that includes naughty cats and little mice!"

Santa waved his fingers and as if by magic Mr T toddled off to his basket, turned round three times and fell fast asleep. "Now little fellow it's your turn," he said, and he placed Barnaby at the entrance to his home. "Off to bed now, it's a big day tomorrow!"

"Night night Santa," yawned Barnaby. "Merry Christmas!"

"And a Happy Christmas to you! Good night, Barnaby," said Santa, and then in a puff of smoke he was gone! Barnaby crept into bed and soon fell fast asleep.

Next morning when the mice woke up imagine their surprise for there hanging at the bottom of their beds were stockings crammed full of presents. In the corner of the room sat a tiny Christmas tree decorated with tinsel and baubles and on the top the most beautiful fairy with gossamer wings. She was wearing a silvery dress that shimmered and sparkled and was just the right size for a little mouse called Bernadette.

THE NIGHT BEFORE CHRISTMAS

Ella Atherton

James crept downstairs, his step-father told him he risked death by hanging if he dared to get out of bed before six o'clock on Christmas morning. James wasn't sure if his step-father was joking or not. He thought not because he never made empty threats.

The delicious smell of newly baked minced pies and home-made ginger wine filled the house and James' nostrils. His mother had worked hard preparing for Christmas day and James was looking forward to Grandma Kizzy and Uncle Malcolm coming for lunch. He knew Uncle Malcolm wasn't his real uncle. He'd been his real daddy's best friend and because he didn't have a family of his own, he loved Mummy's cooking and was always the first to arrive. Especially for Christmas lunch. Malcolm always brought great presents and was so funny signing cracker jokes. His signing was good but not the best and he made James laugh so much it set them all off. All except James' step-father who refused to learn sign language. He would wear a stern look of disapproval. He seemed to disapprove of everything James and his mother did and that disapproval usually extended to his wife's family too. James' sign name for his step-father was 'Downward Mouth' because he never smiled.

James' knew that his step-father wanted to send him to a school for the deaf in Edinburgh. James' mother refused. She said it was too far away, James wouldn't be happy living away from home and she would miss him too much. Besides, the local school had made excellent provision for James and the teachers and many of the children had learned sign language. She said she wished he could be more understanding and learn sign language too. James' step-father was adamant that James should be sent away and became incandescent with rage during these arguments, especially when his wife started to cry.

*

Despite Downward Mouth's disapproval and threats of hanging, James felt giddy with excitement as he opened the living room door, wedging it back with the pussycat doorstop to allow residual light from the hall illuminate the living room. He guessed his mother had switched off the tree lights before going to bed but the tree still looked stunning; decked in silver and gold tinsel and the paper decorations James had made with such enthusiasm at school. James was fascinated by the shapes wrapped in Christmas paper and placed according to size beneath the tree. His step-father said Mummy was OCD. James didn't know what that meant but he loved the symmetry of the presents under the tree, even though he wasn't really sure what that meant either. He thought everything his mother did was perfect and very 'artistic'; a word Miss Bellamy frequently signed to describe James' drawings in art appreciation. James felt a sizzle of anticipation as he knelt beneath the tree and began to feel the mysterious shapes wrapped in a kaleidoscope of coloured paper. He thought he recognised some of the contents, a soft and squidgy parcel was probably a jumper or something to wear anyway.

The next parcel felt like a skate board and another like a Transformer and so on until he came to a small, box-like shape wrapped in gold paper. It was very heavy. James shook the box but nothing moved. There wasn't a label on the box but James assumed it was for him. He was consumed with curiosity and proceeded to open the mysterious parcel. He carefully removed the sticky tape, before peeling back the paper to reveal a dark brown box with a gold clasp. He set the box on the floor and after several attempts managed to release the clasp. James was 'gob-smacked' - another favourite sign of Malcolm's - when he saw that the box contained a small handgun. James' eyes lit up. He'd asked for a Nerf Super Soaker but had never in his wildest dreams thought he'd get a real gun. The gun was impressive, beautifully crafted with a curlicue 'M' etched on the wooden handle. James took the gun from its moulded compartment marvelling at its weight and mesmerised by the light from the hall glinting on the barrel. He held the gun in both hands. The gun was so heavy he could barely keep his hands from shaking. He curled his fingers around the trigger and pressed. Nothing happened. He scrutinised the mechanism until he found a little release button which he pressed, just as his step-father stormed into the room.

'I told you not to get out of bed before six o'clock you little sod,' said Downward Mouth, brandishing a rope. Although James didn't understand the words he had no trouble in reading his step-father's angry face and possible intentions. James leapt to his feet inadvertently squeezing the trigger as he did so. Downward Mouth's expression turned from anger to sheer horror as he clutched his belly before sinking to the living room floor. James didn't understand what had happened. He thought Downward Mouth must have tripped. Then he saw blood oozing from the middle of his step-father's body. James stood frozen in terror until his mother ran into the room. She looked from James to her husband, her face changed from bewilderment to the shape of a scream. She ran to James' step-father, whose eyes were wide-open but rapidly glazing over. He was bleeding out. James' mother grabbed a cushion from the sofa and pressed it into her husband's stomach. She prized the gun from James' clawed hand and signed that he should press down on the cushion - to stem the blood flow - until she came back. James did as his mother said until she returned moments later and told him she had called an ambulance and he should go to his room immediately.

*

James sat in his room, waiting for his mother to tell him what had happened and what was wrong with his step-father. He sat for what felt like hours until overcome with cold and exhaustion, he crept under his Spiderman duvet and curled into a foetal ball. It was almost light when his bedroom door opened and Sarah, the sign language translator from school came in followed by a woman in a police uniform. James signed 'hello' to Sarah and asked her what was happening.

'I am so, so sorry, James,' signed Sarah. 'They couldn't save your step-father; he died on the way to hospital'. She told him the police had questioned his mother and now this 'nice lady' wanted to ask him some questions too.

'Don't worry,' signed Sarah, 'everything will be all right.'

Through Sarah, the policewoman asked James to tell her what happened and to start at the beginning from the moment he decided to go downstairs. James told her everything he could remember but missed out the part about his step-father threatening to hang him. The policewoman listened to Sarah's translation very carefully, letting James tell his story without interruption, before asking him specific questions. At the end of the interview the policewoman said it was quite clearly an accident.

'Do you have any questions for me James?' she asked.

'Yes,' he signed. 'Has Santa been and when can I have my gun back?'

CRACK ON CHRISTMAS

Nick Robinson

Snow fell outside, drifting down and settling on the thick tavern windowsills. Hector, Ralph and Spider stared out through the foggy glass at the sudden invasion and looked down mournfully at their half empty pints. 'It's here again!' Hector finally said.

Ralph refocused, as if coming out of the snow storm itself, and muttered, 'And here's to another year of merry festivities,' raising his glass and rotating his arm in a mocking salute. 'I see that those Smith boys have put up a huge neon Homer Simpson dressed as Santa on their house. Have they not got anything more appropriate to put up than that?'

Spider pulled himself round. 'Yeah, Christmas seems to be so cheap and cheesy these days. We can't even use a character from a country that celebrates Christmas properly. I see we've gone all in on America's Black Friday fiasco too getting all those young mums scrambling for their credit cards. Why is it everything that happens over there we have to have to sign up for as well?'

Hector listened to what he had started. 'Aye, but it's not all bad lads, think of that roaring fire, food to feed the five thousand and meeting up with the family. It's the only time of the year most get to meet up. Besides we all need a holiday break at this arctic time of year.'

Ralph and Spider looked at him for a second and both began to chuckle.

'Have you been on that Winter Warmer again! You don't really believe that tripe do you?' Spider retorted. 'Christmas is such a joke hijacked by capitalist crazies to make us over-spend and suffer financially. Anyways, who says that anyone really wants to meet up with relatives? Do you really want to see Grandad dribble on his Brussels, and Auntie Bet talk endlessly about quality produce at *Waitrose*?'

Ralph ripped in too. 'What about all those people that haven't got any family, they must be having a whale of a time at Christmas - toasting themselves, cooking their own Iceland bought turkey crown and pulling both ends of the cracker at the same time. What a day that must be!'

Hector put down his pint 'You two are missing the point entirely - where's your Christmas spirit? It's a time for giving and seeing all the kids' eyes light up when they open their presents! A time for switching on the Christmas lights on the tree and getting together with other folk to celebrate. All those bells, reindeer and decorations must do something for your Christmas soul?'

Spider drained his glass. 'All I see is the little tykes getting fatter and fatter after every *Quality Street*. It seems to be teaching them that they should expect a whole host of expensive presents and for what? Just because it's the silly season. In my day I got a tangerine and a copy of the *Dandy* and was glad of it! It's greed, greed and more greed these days! What values does this teach the next generation? The generation which will be looking after us in our old age?'

Ralph had been to the bar to gather the next round, the frothy beer spilling onto the shiny table, and he sighed. He pulled out his cigarettes and pointed to the dark, white covered world outside. 'You coming?' motioning to Spider. Both men were gone in seconds, leaving Hector to his pint.

Outside, the cold was biting, and they gathered their thick coats around their robust bodies. The breeze made the snowflakes dance in wave-like motions, before hitting the ground. In the air there was something... a faraway sound, no not a *sound* – singing, and as they puffed and pulled on their cigarettes, the singing became louder and clearer. The men became interested as the quality of the singing became apparent, and they moved forward. It was as if their legs had a mind of their own, and now felt unfazed by the freezing conditions. As they turned the corner at the back of the *Bear and Bishop* they worked their way down the small road and found the source of the singing on the cross-section.

In the glow of a street light, Carol singers gathered, and as the snow drifted and settled, they sang the most harmonious and delightful songs the men had ever heard. It was as if each Carol singer was an angel covered in silver light, while everything else lay dark and drab.

The men stood transfixed, and as the singing continued each thought back to happier times when they too were young and carefree at Christmas. A time of joyous laughter in happy homes, and the smell of Christmas pud, and gravy in the tin. A simpler time when communities came together to celebrate the Glad Tidings. The Carols continued, and the gathering grew as more and more people joined in to listen. Snow gathered on their shoulders but it was in their hearts the ice melted, and Christmas became relevant once more.

It was only much later the pair sheepishly made their way back and found Hector still firmly wedged to his seat.

He eyed them curiously. 'That must have been the longest cigarette break ever?' he remarked, but he found the pair lost for words, rosy cheeked and smiling from ear to ear. 'So, let's have it? Why the Cheshire cat grins?'

Spider was the first to find his voice but all he could say was 'And a very happy Christmas to you, Hector my dear fellow!' followed by Ralph ranting on about how he was going to make home-made brandy butter to go with the pudding this year and how they were all invited.

Hector looked bewildered, but took it all in good grace, accepting the winter warmer they both forced upon him.

It was indeed a *marvellous time* for most at Christmas, he thought to himself, with a grin.

IS SANTA REAL?

Pat Harkness

Do you remember when you were seven or eight?
Shouting up the chimney? Oh, wasn't it great?
Asking Santa on Christmas Eve
For all your presents for him to leave
On Christmas morning, early and bright
and how you couldn't sleep at all that night.
But is Santa real we hear you ask
And does he still complete his task?
Well, when you hear the tinkle of a bell
That's Santa's way of saying that all is well.
After all these years, let us not forget
The magic of Christmas, so please don't fret
Leave a mince pie, a glass of rum or perhaps gin;
If they're gone in the morning, then you know it was him!
Let us wish for peace and goodwill to all
As so many have done in the days of yore.
Remember, too, the baby born in times gone by
Let us hope for that magic as Christmas draws nigh
Listen for the bell: shh – did you hear it then?
Santa is real, and he will come again.
We hope that this message will bring you good cheer
As we wish you a Merry Christmas and a Happy New Year!

OH LITTLE TOWN OF BOTCHERBY

Len Docherty

It was Christmas Eve, and Joseph and Mary Good were packing up the car. They were preparing to travel from their home in Newcastle, to spend Christmas with friends in West Cumbria. Joseph said if they set off after lunch, and had a stop at the *Little Chef* on the A69, they would be at their friends by early evening.

Mary was pregnant, but the baby wasn't due until mid- January. She was struggling and wasn't sure she would be fit to travel. Joseph was desperate to see their friends, and assured her she would be fine by Christmas Eve. She put on a brave face, but would still rather have stayed at home. However, she knew that Joseph was very much the boss, and wouldn't take no for an answer. She had wished for a Christmas baby, but though disappointed, couldn't wait for its arrival.

Mary made lunch, but picked at her food, and had to rush to the toilet. When she returned, Joseph wasn't happy, and accused her of feigning sickness. She broke down and sobbed; telling Joseph, that it was alright for him; as he didn't have to suffer with everything pregnancy brings. He pooh-poohed this, and went to finish packing the car.

Before getting in the car, Mary filled a hot water bottle, to help her tummy. Joseph wasn't impressed, but for once, kept quiet. It was a sunny, frosty, winter day, but the roads had been gritted. They travelled in silence; Joseph attentive to road conditions; Mary just happy to be left alone.

In no time at all, they reached the *Little Chef* and got out, although Mary would happily have had forty winks. Joseph ate hungrily; Mary managed a coffee and a small biscuit. Joseph asked if she was improving, she said yes. The café was full of boisterous workers, breaking up for the festive season, and Mary longed for the silence of the car.

They set off again, and Mary dropped off to sleep, much to Joseph's disgust. He switched the radio on, but could only find Radio 1, so he switched it off again. Mary woke up with a start, as the car came to a shuddering halt. She asked what was wrong; Joseph said a pheasant had run it in front of the car, and he'd had to brake. The sudden braking of the car had upset Mary's tummy again, and much to Joseph's disgust, she leapt out, and was almost sick. She got back in, and Joseph, with total disregard, put the foot down, and shot off down the road.

Darkness had set in, and Mary asked Joseph to put the heater on. He muttered under his breath, but did turn the heating on: not very hot. When they arrived at Brampton, Mary needed the toilet, and Joseph stopped while she entered a hotel. They started off again, and were soon on the outskirts of Carlisle. Mary's tummy pains had returned, as the hot water bottle was now cold. She was desperate to stop, but was too scared to ask Joseph.

They passed *Tesco*, just after coming over junction 43, and her pains were getting more severe. She started to rock with the pain, and Joseph for once, looked a worried man. "Do you need to stop love? You look dreadful, and I'm sorry for the way I've treated you." Mary looked at Joseph, and told him she needed to find somewhere to get help. They had only travelled a further hundred yards, when they were passing a side road. Just off this road, there was an old school, and the playground was bathed in bright lights. They turned onto the side road, and Joseph turned off the engine. He got out of the car and went towards the light. It was a Christmas nativity play; played out by local youngsters. There was a crib containing a doll; also children playing Mary and Joseph, and the three wise men. There were also a number of adults, and even a real donkey and a small lamb.

The crowd were suddenly aware of Joseph's presence, and his urgency. He asked if there were any medical people at the play, as his wife wasn't very well. A couple of ladies rushed forward, and said they were both paramedics, and were willing to help. Joseph took them to his car, and explained his wife's condition. They asked him to move the car nearer to the school, so that it would be easier to tend his wife. He did so, and in no time Mary was removed from the car, and rushed into the old school building. The women explained that it was currently the local Community Centre. Mary was taken into the kitchen, and Joseph was ushered out, as it was women's business.

Joseph realised that Mary was in good hands and went out to watch the nativity play. He was impressed by the professionalism and maturity of the youngsters, and for a while, he forgot about Mary. He noticed a bright light, and noticed it was a bright star shining on the players. Unconsciously, his mind started to go back in time: to the original nativity: Mary and Joseph, and the birth of Jesus. Was the bright star sending him a message? He was jolted out of his thoughts by an infant's cry, and he ran into the Community Centre. He opened the kitchen door, and saw Mary, holding a tiny new born baby. He forgot he was a grown man, and the tears ran down his cheeks. He hugged Mary, and turning round, hugged the two paramedics.

"I... we... can't thank you enough for all your wonderful attention." He took the new born from Mary and cuddled it.

"We were only too happy to help out. After all, it is Christmas, the time of goodwill to everyone. By the way, I'm Sue, and this is my friend Heather, and as we haven't told you yet, you have a baby son!"

"Thank you, both," Mary said, "shame it's a boy, we could have named it Sue and Heather."

"Thanks for the kind thoughts, but Christmas is all about a certain little boy," Sue said, and she and Heather wished the happy couple Happy Christmas and returned to watch the play.

"Let's go outside and show off our new arrival." Mary said. Joseph agreed, and they went outside.

Everyone cheered, and the young Joseph came up to them. He was quite bashful, but after his Mum prompted him, he asked if the new baby boy, could replace the doll in the crib. Mary and Joseph felt they couldn't refuse, and duly placed him in the crib. They then announced that their baby son had to be named Jesus, and everyone cheered.

The three wise men came to the crib, and each gave Jesus a gift. A box of *Maltesers,* a box of *Liquorice Allsorts* and finally a box of *Terry's All Gold.* The night was frosty, moonlit and silent, but it was to end in style. The silence was broken by a tiny infant's cry, and a modern day Jesus announced himself to the world.

THE SURPRISE

Neil Robinson

It wasn't until they were a couple of hundred miles from home that his parents realised neither of them had packed his Christmas present.

They'd stopped at a service station on the M6 and while Dylan scrambled out of the cold into the back of the car, still clutching the bag with his books and sweets in, his mum and dad began to argue. He watched them through the windscreen, their warm breath cloudy in the icy air, his mum waving a polystyrene coffee cup around. He couldn't really make out what they were saying, but he didn't care. They were arguing again.

"I thought you'd put it in," his mum said.

'"You were doing the packing," his dad snapped back.

"Oh, that's right. Blame me. As if I didn't have enough to do," his mum said.

Dylan rummaged in his bag for another mint, moving aside everything else in the old school satchel, and popped the sweet in his mouth. He hoped if it would start to snow. Wasn't that what was supposed to happen on Christmas Eve?

"It's out of the question," his dad was saying now. "We are not going back. No. Not 200 miles."

They were on their way to his gran's for the holiday. Dylan hadn't wanted to go; he liked being at home on Christmas Day, but it was their turn to visit his grandparents, all the way up in Carlisle, so that's what they were doing.

"He'll just have to wait until we get home. That's all there is to it", dad said.

"He's going to be so upset," said his mum. "I can't see to everything."

His parents got back in the car and they set off again. Dad put the radio on. A nice Scottish sounding lady was playing Christmas songs. 'Christmas is forgiving and forgetting,' said the song they could hear as they pulled back on to the motorway.

"This'll cheer us up," dad said, smiling at Dylan through the mirror, though Dylan didn't really feel like he needed cheering up.

There were wisps of snow in the air as they pulled up at gran and granddad's. Dylan had fallen asleep for the last part of the journey and was surprised when he woke to see how dark it was, even though it was still only the afternoon. Already the houses in the road had their Christmas tree lights on. Something told him it was going to be a lovely Christmas after all, even if he was a long way from home. He was sure too that Santa would know where he was and would remember to deliver his presents to his grandparents' house instead of his own.

Gran made the usual fuss of him when they went in and he did his best to let her. She had flour on her cheek and the house smelt of mince pies and Christmas tree. Gran still liked a real one. The one they had at home was made of silver tinsel. Granddad appeared, all jolly and with a mouthful of mince pie. He ruffled Dylan's hair, which he didn't really like, and said, "come through and warm yourselves up," spraying little bits of pastry into the air so that Gran flicked the tea towel at him and told him off for eating the mince pies she'd just made. Dylan and his mum went through to the living room where the Christmas tree looked lovely, all twinkly and sparkly, while dad brought the bags in from the car.

After tea they watched a funny programme on the television, Dylan clutching his precious bag, until it was time for bed.

His mum came up to tuck him in. "You know," she said, "sometimes we don't... we don't always get what we're expecting at Christmas. Sometimes we have to wait a little longer..."

Dylan looked up at her. "I know that," he said. "But I'm sure Santa won't let me down. I know he won't, mum."

His mother gulped. "Just so you're prepared," she said. "Just in case."

"Don't worry," he said. "I'm sure everything will be all right." His mum seemed to be all snuffly, but she kissed him on the forehead and said, "Good night, darling," before going back downstairs.

He couldn't sleep of course and later, through the wall, could hear his mum and dad's voices from the next bedroom.

"He'll feel we've let him down," his mother sobbed.

"It's only a SmartPad, for goodness sake," his dad said all low and grumbly. "It's not the end of the world."

"I wouldn't care," his mum said, "but I wrapped it and left it all ready to pick up before we left."

"He'll have it in a few days," his dad said. "Don't worry." It went quiet after that. Dylan could imagine them getting all sloppy, so he took a comic out of his bag and began to read.

He didn't get up early next morning, Christmas Day itself. He might have done if he'd been at home, but he had been awake in the night, excited about his presents and the big surprise he knew was coming. He waited until he heard gran in the bathroom before slipping on his dressing gown and going downstairs. He flicked on the switch for the Christmas tree lights so they lit up the room and there, under the tree, were his presents – the ones from gran and granddad and those his parents had remembered – together with everyone else's. He knelt down in front of them, all wrapped in brightly coloured paper with gift-tags and bows, and looked for the one he was sure was his special present.

"Let me explain," his mother said from the doorway, "You see, your dad..."

"Look, mum," Dylan exclaimed, interrupting her. "It's the SmartPad I asked for. Santa's brought it."

Mum blinked tearfully at her son and looked accusingly at her husband. "I don't understand," she said, "How can...?"

"I told you," said Dylan, beaming widely and tearing the final scraps of wrapping paper from the SmartPad box. "Santa did it, like he always does."

Gran muttered something about 'scarlet ribbons', which made no sense to anyone, and Dylan thought of his bag; the little brown satchel that always – *always* – kept his secrets.

THE LEADER OF THE PACK

Pat Harkness

It was Boxing Day teatime and the year was 1961. My family were sprawled in the sitting room comatose with too much food, and one too many sherries. The vestibule door opened and male voices could be heard but we paid no mind. A few minutes later, Nana came bustling in. "You're not going to believe this," she exclaimed, "but there's a big ginger-haired lad in there, and he's leaning on the mantelpiece!" None of us could even reach the mantelpiece!

"Oh no, not him again!" I said as I stormed into the living room, I had crossed swords with this toe-rag before. His gang were helping themselves to the leftovers, and sure enough their leader was indeed leaning on the mantelpiece.

He was six feet tall and lean, with a mop of unruly red hair and sideboards down to his chin and was dressed in black sweater, tight black jeans, a wide leather belt studded with copper rivets, winkle picker shoes and he dominated the room. Leering at me he said, "Hi, Pat! Me and the lads have come to wish you a Merry Christmas!" The 'lads' shouted out a Christmas greeting.

I pulled myself up to my full height of five feet, one and three quarter inches. "Well you have," I hissed, "so hop it!"

"S'not very friendly, let the lads have a drink," said Dad, the inebriate.

"They're only seventeen, Dad, same as me. They shouldn't be drinking!" I glared at them.

Keith, he of the mantelpiece, said "That's okay, we're off to a party at Longsowerby anyway," then strutting across the room he patted me on the bottom and with a chorus of 'See ya later, Alligator,' they all went off into the night.

New Year's Eve was on a Sunday and the dances didn't start until midnight. Mam had made me a turquoise and white full skirted cotton dress made even fuller by the sugar-starched net underskirts. I was wearing huge white poppit-beads, white stilettos, off-white swagger coat and the ensemble was completed by my bouffant hairstyle and bright pink lipstick. I was ready to party and dance the night away at Bonds Dance Hall.

We left the party in Harraby around 10.30 to walk into the city centre. Carlisle was bathed in a blanket of snow which sparkled and glistened under the lamplight and looked so beautiful. We paired up on the way, as only couples were allowed into the dance, and spirits were high as we arrived in Fisher Street to join the queue.

After waiting a while I heard a voice "Pat! Hi, how ya doing?" I groaned but there he was, bold as brass, pushing his way through the crowd towards me. I tried to make myself invisible but it was to no avail.

He stopped, picked me up, swung me round and planted a smacker of a kiss on my cheek. "A kiss for Christmas," he said.

"Get off," I demanded "put me down."

"What about a kiss for New Year?" he said and kissed me again! The nerve of the guy! I hit him and wriggled free, my partner mumbling "She's with me," to the response "Beat it, pipsqueak!"

Then turning to me he said "I know, how about a kiss for Easter?" I giggled in spite of myself, and was promptly hoisted up again - this time the kiss was gentle.

Excitement mounted as the queue moved forward, but at ten to twelve Big Tom the doorman came out "I'm so sorry, lads and lasses, but we're full up." There were moans and groans from the remaining crowd, but it soon disappeared.

I was now faced with a long walk home in the freezing cold.

"Want a lift, Shorty? The glow from the streetlight onto a head of burnished copper was a clear indication as to the owner of the voice. "You'll need this then," he said and plonked a crash helmet on my head.

"What the…?"

"Come on," he said as I stared in disbelief at the Lambretta scooter parked on the side of the road. "Hop on!"

I climbed on demurely, sitting side-saddle so as not to crease my dress. We drove off into Finkle Street turning into Castle Street. There was an eerie silence broken only by the noise of the engine, the snow like fluffy white pillows as we headed towards the Town Hall. At Richard's shop, the scooter toppled over and we both fell onto the soft snow. Keith was back on his feet right away "Well, don't mess about, jump on!" I climbed on, straddling the bike giving no thought to decorum.

As we turned towards the Viaduct, the snow had changed into dark brown slush, and as we passed the Central Hotel, the scooter went into a skid. I was thrown off, landed on my back and slid across the road. Bike and rider went careering down the hill.

"Help, help!" I shouted, thrashing my arms and legs about. "I can't get up, help!"

A taxi driver came to my aid. "Are you all right, love?" Was I all right? I was bruised, battered, filthy, and soaked to the skin. And where was my knight in shining armour? Why, calmly examining his bike!

On spotting me he said, "I think she's okay."

"Oh, goody!" I said sarcastically, for neither he nor his damned bike was going to get the better of me. I climbed back on.

By the time we arrived in Richardson Street, we were purple and shivering with cold. We went inside our teeth chattering. Keith banked the fire up, and I made a cup of tea. We stood, dripping, drank our tea, and talked. We cuddled, we kissed, and then talked some more, and I was sitting on his knee when we heard the front door open. "It's my Mam and Dad," I said panicking. "Let me up!"

"Only if you'll go out with me tomorrow night," he said holding me tight.

"I can't," I started to say, but he didn't let go. "Yes, yes, okay" and I just made it to the empty chair.

The door opened and Mam switched on the light. We were like two rabbits trapped in the headlights.

"Happy New Year, Mam and Dad!" I said weakly.

"And what's been going on here?" Mam demanded.

"I fell…" I started to say, but Keith butted in.

"Yes, Pat fell in the snow, so I thought I'd walk her home."

She ignored him. "You weren't on that bike were you?"

"No, no," said Keith. "It wouldn't have been safe in this weather. We just walked, didn't we, Pat?"

I just nodded, and it was then that I noticed my tattered stockings, my limp, filthy party dress, my poppit beads had popped and my hair! Oh Lord! Mam was not amused, but Dad, full of New Year cheer, was grinning like a Cheshire cat.

After sizing up the situation Keith said, "Well, I'd best be off. Happy New Year, Mr Long!" he said shaking Dad's hand, and then, to our amazement, he lifted my mother up, planted a kiss on her cheek and said "Happy New Year, Nellie!" and with, "I'll see you later!" he was gone.

I gawped, my Dad chuckled, but Mam was speechless. *My Mam speechless!* Eventually she spluttered, "We- we-well, the cheeky monkey!"

Yes, he was! And that was why I fell for - the leader of the pack.

A CHRISTMAS STORY

Ella Atherton

After watching *Star Wars* and *The Grinch* at Christmas for the third time, Robbie thought he should get some fresh air and decided to go into town and have a look at the Christmas lights. He hoisted himself out of his computer chair and into his hand-controlled wheelchair. He missed his electronic wheelchair but the police and social services told him it would be safer for everyone if he had a hand-operated one. Robbie knew they blamed him for George Graham's unfortunate demise when he clipped the wheel of George's silver racer on Eden Bridges. Robbie always maintained it was an accident even though witnesses said they saw him laughing when George and his bike executed that perfect arc over the parapet into the swollen Eden below. Robbie swore he wasn't laughing, 'It was a grimace,' he told the coroner. He had no idea where that word came from other than it started out in his head as 'grin' but he managed to change it before it came out of his mouth.

Well, that was in year eleven. Robbie was glad to be in the sixth form now and he was looking forward to a much brighter future though not a very bright Christmas.

Still, things could be worse and using a manual chair had improved Robbie's upper body strength to the point where he liked to admire himself in the mirror as he flexed his biceps.

'Look at them bad boys,' he said to his reflection.

'What bad boys?' asked his mother as she came crashing into his bedroom.

'Don't you ever knock?'

'This is my house, why should I knock?'

'Because I'm not a kid. I need privacy.'

'You'll always be a kid to me. My little boy.'

'Oh Mam,' said Robbie in exasperation. 'This is my room. I need privacy and you're drunk.'

'Bit tipsy. Christmas tipple is all,' said Rob's mother as she tripped over his computer cable and landed headlong onto his bed.

'My God, why can't people stay upright around me?'

'Upright, bed-right,' slurred his mother.

'Mam, are you alright?'

'Yes, pet, little sheep... sleep.'

'Right, I'm off,' said Rob, donning his bright red puffa jacket. He left his mother to sleep it off. He knew his Dad would be home soon and he could look after Mam if need be.

Rob was glad as well as proud of his new strength and it didn't take him long to negotiate the ramp out of the front door, before making his way up the hill to Stanwix Village. He zoomed down the hill past the Chinese Gardens, across Eden Bridges, past the Sand's Centre, through Hardwicke Circus, past the Civic Centre and up the short incline into Scotch Street with its display of Christmas lights. The smell of sausage rolls, fish and chips, coffee and even soap products added to Rob's excitement as he made his way to English Street and the town hall square.

There was a festive feeling in town as shoppers bustled from shop to shop laden with Christmas parcels. Robbie stopped his chair under the Old Town Hall with its suspended net of gold and white twinkling lights. He was looking at the chocolates in a shop window when he was approached by two men. One in a Santa outfit and the shorter man was dressed as an elf in a little green suit. The elf looked vaguely familiar.

'Excuse me, son,' said Santa. 'Can you tell me the way to the Old Town Hall?'

Rob was about to tell him he'd reached his destination when he saw the pity in his eyes. He was fed up of being patronised just because he was a wheelchair-user. He shrugged his shoulders and in his best French said, *'Je ne comprends pas,'* (I do not understand) followed by, *'sling yourself and your elf,'* in equally good French. Oblivious to the insult, Santa turned away to find someone more helpful. The elf stayed for a moment and with a twinkle in his eye wished Rob, *'Bon Noel!'* in perfect French before throwing a handful of silver glitter.

'Magic Dust,' he said. 'Feel free to make a wish.'

Rob scorned the idea of Magic Dust as he steered his chair to the band stand that was strung with fairy lights, where the Salvation Army were playing Christmas carols. Robbie thought he would take a look at the big tree sent over from Norway each year and maybe the white angels and the three kings from orient-are. He was bitterly disappointed when he turned the corner to find neither the angels nor the kings.

Rob's disappointment was short-lived and he found himself singing along with the Sally Army, 'O come all ye faithful, joyful and triumphant.' Besides, he was used to greater disappointments in his life, not least his lack of female companionship.

Cynthia Bowman had been Rob's companion throughout school, but he always thought she was more interested in practising her social work skills rather than any real interest in him. Anyway, they'd grown apart after he killed George Graham. Well, he didn't really kill George but he let the school bullies think he had. They were more cautious of him now. Especially when George's body was found in the Solway Firth. The bullying stopped completely.

Rob's biggest disappointment this year was the lack of party invitations. His one sustaining thought was that Cynthia had given up the idea of social work and had applied to Loughborough to study engineering. Rob had also applied to Loughborough to read sports science. He was encouraged by his favourite teacher, Joe Lowe, who recognised Rob's new upper body strength and introduced him to wheelchair racing. Rob's greatest wish was to compete in the next Paralympics and to have a proper relationship with Cynthia.

Rob's heart fluttered when he thought of Cynthia and almost burst out of his chest when he actually saw her coming towards him near the big toy shop. She was wearing her own version of a Goth outfit; a long black dress swathed in red and gold Christmas garlands. Her hair was tied up in silver ribbons, little tendrils loose around her adorable face. She even had flashing Christmas pudding earrings and instead of black boots, she was wearing fluffy white moon boots. The sight of her warmed Rob deep within the cockles of his heart, or maybe even south of that region…

Cynthia hailed Rob with a bottle of sparkling wine:

'Hey Rob. Come on, I'm going to a party at the student house on Abbey Street. You're invited.'

Rob's heart leapt with joy as Cyn jumped on to the back of his wheelchair to hitch a ride. Just as she used to when they were in year eleven together. He and Cyn sped down Castle Street, past the Cathedral lit up in all its Christmas glory. The sound of the choir singing carols echoed in the crisp night air.

'Get yourself some wheels', shouted Cyn to a gawping passers-by, as she wrapped her Christmas garland around Rob's shoulders before leaning forward to kiss him gently on the cheek.

Rob's heart rejoiced.

'Thank you, Mr Elf,' he shouted, 'for making my Christmas wish come true!'

'Mr Elf?' queried Cyn. 'What are you on about?'

'Oh, just a Warwick Davis look-alike,' he laughed, as they sped towards the Christmas party and the rest of their lives.

SNOWFLAKES

Susan Cartwright-Smith

I find it strange, in this day and age,
That compassion and a rational way of wanting change
For people who are different or estranged
Is seen as dangerous, or odd.
We are called Snowflakes, those of us who feel
That taking more than needed is greedy, or unfeeling,
Ignoring plights of needy souls, who are not very different
From us. And our role in society
Is to make sure all are catered for. The hatred spewed by lewd and tawdry
Newspapers we manage to blank out, and not take notice.
But this makes us "special", and even worse, "caring".
Daring to suggest, that frankly we are drowning in
Possessions we don't need and wasting food
While others drown for colour or for creed, who *we could feed.*
To be a Snowflake, therefore,
Is somehow weak, only a freak would bother
With the sake of someone who is not their own.
We resist, and want the moaning bores who say
"PC gone mad" to stop, desist, but they persist.
Why is it bad to care? As if to dare
To show a little understanding
Is too hard, just so demanding, as if
Equality is bad for me. I'm not grandstanding,
I just cannot see why it is wrong.
To show you care about another, who ain't your brother,
Mother, friend or sometime lover, who you've never met, will never meet,
They don't live along your street, you won't go in their shelter, tent or cardboard box,
Won't go to clubs they frequent, you won't find your time spent

In their halls of worship, beauty parlours, cafes, or be subjected to the shocks
That they endure just for who they are.
They might not live like your or my way, but you kind of want them
To be okay. It isn't fey.
As seen today, if snowflakes gather
Join together, fall at once, they change the world.
They cover up the dogsh*t, smooth out creases,
Cover tangled mess of gardens left unchecked,
And it pleases everyone to see a quietened world.
I suspect that snow makes everyone feel slow,
We cannot rush, the world has hush, we might have to
Change in which direction we planned to go.
It quietens the chaos of the everyday, with noiseless beauty.
There is so much to say on both sides of debate,
Anger, fear, the ebb and flow
Of tides of right and wrong and right and left,
By those bereft, and those whose fight seems out of date,
The spate of killings makes no sense to those of us
Who do not carry. They condone violence? We can't keep our silence.
There are so many causes, Snowflakes seem on constant flurry
With no pauses, while common sense is buried under
Soundbites, and tense arguments. The incidents of hate crime,
Gun crime and the meanness and uncharity
From those who claim religious piety. So you see
I see no shame in Snowflakes. I am not lame to be PC
And I am yet to melt. I will gather those to me
Who fight, believe in rights, the right to love, the right to heal, the right to live
And form a furious blizzard.
Freeze the breath on hateful tongues, quieten the psalm from hypocrites,
Be the balm that soothes the itch of change.
Be brave. It is not strange, I call my snowflake friends to arms -
Let's cover this beautiful world with calm.

FIRST CHRISTMAS

Neil Robinson

Mary sat shivering in the corner. It had been a terrible journey. She was cold and wet and could feel the baby moving inside her. She knew it wouldn't be long before he'd be born and of course she'd always known it was going to be a boy. Joe reappeared with a cup of steaming something and handed it to her.

'Here, drink this,' he said, 'it'll warm you up.' He put his arm round her and pulled her close. She smiled weakly at him and took a sip; some sort of herbal concoction, bitter and sweet at the same time. Joe lifted the shawl back round her shoulders. She wished she was at home and that they hadn't risked the journey, not at this time of year and in her condition. Now here they were on the outskirts of the town Joe's family had originally come from and a long way from their village and the little house they'd set up together.

He took the cup from her as she felt the first of her pains and said he'd go and find the landlady to help her with the birth. She'd said she would when they arrived, apologising that because of the time of year and the big occasion that had brought everyone into town she couldn't offer them one of her decent rooms; they were all taken, she explained, except the one they now found themselves in. It was cold and had no running water, but was still far better than being outside where the mist was now thicker and icier than it had been only minutes earlier.

'Hello?' Joe called out across the yard, 'Can you give us a hand here?' The landlady, who'd introduced herself as Beth King, scurried from the kitchen of the main house, wiping her hands on her apron. The mist parted like the red sea as she passed through it.

'Is it time?' she said. 'I'll fetch the towels and hot water.' Joe had never known why these things were necessary whenever a baby was about to be born but, as they were always called for, he guessed they must be. Beth disappeared again into the swirling fog, emerging again moments later with what turned out to be a box of towels and cloths, followed by Mr King with an urn of scalding water.

'Now don't you men get in the way,' Mrs King commanded, taking charge. 'Make yourselves useful by...' she paused as she helped Mary make herself more comfortable, 'by making yourselves scarce.'

'C'mon son,' Mr King said to Joe. 'We'll leave them to it. Come and warm yourself up in the kitchen.' Joe had thought he wanted to be with Mary as she brought their son into the world, and was shocked, now it came to it, at how easily he allowed himself to be talked out of it.

'You go,' Mary said, teeth chattering. 'We'll manage.' She had reached the point that she didn't care whether he was there or not. She just wanted it over with.

Frank dragged two old chairs across the flagstones and up to the range. He passed Joe another of his herbal infusions. 'Not a night for travelling,' he said.

'No, indeed,' agreed Joe. It was madness really to have attempted it but they'd felt they'd had no choice. They'd felt compelled to make the trip back to the little town from where the Carpenter family hailed. Everything had been fine when they'd left that morning, with a couple of bags each and one for the baby, even though neither of them thought he'd make an appearance quite this early. He wasn't due for another week or two so they were fairly confident they'd be back home before he arrived. It had been a sunny day, if a little chilly, when they'd set off and although Mary found the journey uncomfortable, they were sure they'd arrive before nightfall. But they hadn't counted on the mist that had started to roll in in the late afternoon. Before they knew it, they couldn't see any further than a few feet in front of them, the sides of the road completely obscured. Joe was frightened for his fiancée, her fingers digging deeply into the side of her seat, and for their unborn child. He didn't know what to do; he couldn't stop where they were, wherever that was, but it would be equally dangerous to carry on. So he was relieved when, through the mist, he could just make out the lights from the farm where even now he sat warming himself. Cautiously, he'd steered them down the track towards the building, somehow avoiding the dark, mist-shrouded ditches on either side and reached the farmhouse without incident or accident. Frank answered his desperate knocking and called his wife once he'd explained that, yes, they did usually have rooms, but that on this night, of all nights, they were all taken. 'But you must come in,' Beth had said. 'We can surely sort something, Frank.' And she had fussed about preparing the room in the outhouse, explaining how it wasn't normally used in the winter. But for Joe and Mary it was a godsend, saving them from returning to the road, and a place for Mary finally to rest.

Now, in the drowsy warmth of the kitchen, Frank busied himself stoking the fire and clearing away dishes, while Joe, exhausted after an eventful day, dozed by the fire.

He woke suddenly. A cry from the squat little building outside - a baby's cry. He rushed out into the yard, bumping into Beth in the still swirling mist. 'You have a beautiful baby boy!' she cried. 'Mother and baby both well. Come and see!'

Joe pushed passed her and into the tiny space where Mary and his new son waited for him. He kissed her, feeling guilty, as he had felt so tired himself, about the greater ordeal she had gone through, and picked up the little bundle, the baby wrapped in the towels Beth had insisted on earlier.

'Take him into the house, keep him warm,' she said. 'His mum and I will be there soon.' If, as he crossed the yard again, Joe had looked up he would have seen the solitary light directly above him, moving slowly across the night sky, the only thing visible through thick, clammy fog. Intent instead on the new-born cradled in his arms, a sense of peace such as he'd never known before had overwhelmed him.

He re-entered the kitchen to be met by a veritable host of people: Frank had rounded up his other guests – Mr and Mrs Sheppard and the D'Angelos - to greet the new arrival.

'Oh, he's lovely,' murmured Agnes Sheppard.

'Such a beautiful bambino,' cooed Gabrielle D'Angelo, as heavenly voices drifted through the air, the angels themselves marking the birth of this remarkable baby. On the Welsh dresser, next to the radio from where the strains of *'O Come All Ye Faithful'* came, the kitchen clock showed it was well after after midnight. Christmas Day; Mary and Joe had a Christmas baby.

Mrs King brought Mary into the kitchen and Joe passed their son to her. Agnes produced a toy lamb from somewhere and perched it next to the baby in the crook of Mary's arm. 'It was for my granddaughter,' she said, 'But I can knit her another one.'

'So,' said Mrs King, 'what are you going to call him?'

'Well, there's only one thing I can call him,' Mary said. 'He has to be J.. J... J,' she stammered as nerves and exhaustion finally got the better of her. 'We're going to call him J-Justin,' she said, 'after my favourite singer. Aren't we, Joseph dear?'

CHRISTMAS SPIRIT

John Nevinson

Martin poked his head round the thick white-painted door, and saw that the big lounge was empty, as he had expected. Sighing, he strolled in, and raked the pathetic Christmas tree with critical eyes. Two days before Christmas Day, and already the hotel's fitful central heating was browning the falling pine needles, which coated the floral carpet; the fairy lights had been put on inexpertly, with all the cabling bunched at the bottom of the tree so that very few bulbs were left to glow at the top, where an unstable grubby angel seemed about to topple off at any moment.

"Honestly," Martin thought. "The Atkinsons are absolutely clueless as hotel managers. They still think they're running that third-rate boarding school near Cartmel."

Martin attempted to ease himself into an enormous badly-sprung armchair; it seemed to accept one buttock but not the other, so that he tilted awkwardly as he sank into its tenacious grip. He looked around the dimly-lit lounge critically, knowing that its supposedly classy tables, lamps, oil paintings and chairs had all been purchased in a job-lot from a warehouse near Frizington, which specialised in house-clearances. He remembered once standing with Louisa watching an Aussie ticking off a list of tables, ornaments and bookcases to be shipped out for an English-themed pub in Melbourne.

Ah, Louisa! How many times had they come here for Christmas? They had spent several years unable to leave Carlisle because of her crazy old dad and his crippled mother, but their parents had both died within days of each other one autumn, and as Christmas at home was going to seem so strange and empty that year, Martin and Louisa decided to spoil themselves, and spend the festive season at a hotel in the Lakes. They had chosen the Atkinsons' place near Keswick after Louisa saw it advertised in a Cumbria Life magazine, while under the dryer at *Curl Up and Dye.*

"My Aunty Sissy goes there," announced green-haired Kerri-Ann, "and she says it's nice."

So they had booked in, realised it was Nigel and Hilary Atkinsons' first Christmas running a hotel, and loyally supported the shaky novices by ignoring all the mistakes they made.

"Anyone can undercook a turkey," whispered Louisa, as Martin wondered if they would be heading home early to Carlisle, but only as far as the Cumberland Infirmary.

"Bad luck for them, about the boiler," Martin muttered through chattering teeth as he and Louisa huddled under inadequate summer duvets in a bedroom like a freezer.

They laughed about Overcliffe House when they got home and told friends all about the flickering lights and blocked toilets, but it was grim at the time it happened. Over the years Louisa and Martin had been coming, the guest numbers had unsurprisingly dwindled, and Martin wondered, swallowed up in the chintzy armchair, how long Overcliffe House could last. There didn't seem to be another soul around the building, not even the usual distant sound of Hilary's caterwauling snatches of light opera in the kitchen or Nigel's ex-military bellowing. Martin shivered—it was especially solitary for him as this was his first Christmas without Louisa. He had thought about staying at his big lonely bungalow at Lowry Hill but realised that all his recent happy Christmases had been here at Keswick, and that it would be more comforting to come to failing Overcliffe House, with all its faults.

Still, with nobody to talk to, Martin felt the silence oppressive, and could sense the lack of Louisa's company as painful as a deep unsatisfied hunger. He was about to haul himself from the depths of the chair when the door creaked, and a sharp-featured grey face looked into the room.

"Oh!" The woman looked startled.

"Come in, come in!" ordered Martin and a thin creature in drab clothing tentatively entered the lounge.

"I thought... I thought there was nobody in here..." she began.

"Well, there is!" boomed Martin, coming to life.

"I actually thought there was nobody in the whole building," she smiled nervously.

"Nigel will be in the bowels of the house messing with the boiler controls, and Hilary will be singing away in the kitchen overcooking the dinner," laughed Martin.

"Oh…" Her face fell.

"I am joking. Been coming here for Christmas for years. Eight years. Just joking!"

With a nervous grin, the stick-like woman sidled into an armchair opposite Martin, and he understood her surprise when it seemed to swallow her up into its voluptuous depths.

"Martin Graham," he volunteered.

"Esther Charlton," she said.

There was an uncomfortable silence.

"You come far?" Martin asked. "I am almost local. Carlisle."

"Lancaster," she replied. "Well, nearby anyway. Garstang."

"Oh, not so far. Not Manchester or Newcastle!" he grinned.

Esther smiled demurely, and looked round the room.

"Nice paintings," she observed. "Nice table. Nice…"

As she petered out of "nice" things to say. Martin thought of the dusty warehouse in Frizington where all these "nice" things had been stored.

"Dinner is at six," he announced. "Well, Hilary always aims for six…"

Esther smiled weakly.

"You on your own?" he asked, but it was one question too far for the spinster who reddened as if he had already made an indecent suggestion. Martin realised that Esther thought he had been a bit forward. "My God, it's not 1955. Anyone would assume this was the Fifties. She's in a time warp!" he thought, so he added weakly, "I am alone this year," and knew immediately that this had seemed even more forward, as if hinting that they were two solo guests in a deserted hotel who might become more than that. "Poor woman," he mused. "She thinks she is going to be chased around the hotel all over Christmas!"

"Yes, I am alone," she replied belatedly. "I was supposed to come with my widowed sister but she has had to pull out at the last minute."

"Oh, dear," cooed Martin gently.

"Shingles. She's got shingles," Esther said.

"That's nasty," tutted Martin. "My wife once had it. On her forehead. Nasty thing."

His consideration warmed Esther a little, and she ventured, "You said you are alone. Your wife…?

"I lost Louisa eighteen months ago. July last year. We were here every Christmas."

"I am sorry. How sad for you," Esther smiled shyly. "Doesn't it feel uncomfy to stay here without her?"

"Bless you, not all. Feel quite close to her here, thinking of the happy times we had," he said gruffly.

Martin pulled himself awkwardly from the chair's grip, and walked stiffly to the big bay window looking over Derwentwater. The lake glitterered in the moonlight, as it had been dark for an hour now, and there was just the glow of Keswick's lights shining through the trees below them.

Seeing Esther blink back incipient tears, Martin decided to he needed to lighten the mood. "Happy times, of course----when Hilary wasn't cooking giblets in the plastic bag which was still inside the turkey. Or Nigel fusing the lights!"

Esther smiled and began to laugh, and Martin said, "That's better. Well, it's dinner at six, supposedly, so I'll go and change. See you later!"

He drifted through the door. Esther sat for a moment, and then got up to look around the room. She shook her head at the amateurishly decorated tree and noted its sad condition before standing in the bay window, looking at the trees silhouetted against the lights of the town. She had just noticed it was ten past five on the ornate mantelpiece clock when the door opened.

"Well, hello, Miss Charlton," a bosomy, pink-faced woman boomed breezily as she strode across the lounge. "Nigel said he had booked you in at four o'clock. Sorry. Should have been me who met you but I've been slaving in the galley! I'm the wife. Hilary Atkinson. Is your room okay?"

"Oh, yes, thanks, Mrs Atkinson. I managed to see lovely views from the window just as the sun set."

"Sorry you've been left all alone in here. There is a family arriving from Edinburgh soon. Baxter, I think they are called," said Hilary. "That will liven things up for you!"

"It's good to hear more are staying here other than just Mr Graham and myself," smiled Esther.

"Mr Graham?" asked Hilary.

"Yes. That nice gentleman from Carlisle. Said he used to come here with his wife every Christmas. Wanted to carry on coming even after she passed away."

Hilary's flushed face paled, and she sank into the big armchair.

"Miss Charlton. You were chatting to Martin Graham?" said Hilary weakly.

"Yes, he told me that he didn't mind coming on his own," said Esther. "Happy memories, he said."

"But last year, Miss Charlton. Last year... on Christmas Day morning, Nigel found Martin Graham dead in his bed," gasped Hilary.

Esther was still screaming when the Baxters arrived from Edinburgh.

THE GIFT

Susan Cartwright-Smith

The girl awoke as sleigh bells faded out on the edge of hearing. There was a smell of cold in the air, like an outdoor coat had been hung in the room. She screwed her eyes shut, but slowly they shuttered open again.

She lay staring at the line of light which fell across the end of the bed, from the opened door, casting shadows, illuminating an unfamiliar outline hanging from the footboard.

Her toys were as she had carefully arranged them – dolls and bears fleeing from rampant wooden soldiers, while one liveried monkey primly took tea. Various remembrances and reminiscences of her childhood were pinned to the walls. Time pinned in place, described in paints and crayons.

Do not forget.

She pushed the cover down from her chin, slowly, carefully, cautiously. As the cover travelled down her body she willed herself to sit up, eyes drying with the effort it took to keep them open, fear, attempting to shut them. She blinked. On the edge of sight a flicker in the light told her that someone was watching. Waiting.

They could wait.

She crept to the end of the bed. The stocking which hung there glowed from within with an eerie light. She reached out to retrieve it and was surprised at the weight, considering it was so small.

Upending it, the item rolled out and spilled its light into the room, blinding her against the darkness. She finally looked up into the shadowed face of the person lurking by the door, and tilted her head in silent enquiry, and beckoned him forward.

"It is what you asked for. The only thing you asked for," she heard him say. His voice was not how she had imagined it would be. Gruff, and cracked, like it had not been used often. Or the tongue was unfamiliar in this head.

"I never expected it to weigh so heavy. I am not sure what I expected. I'm not even sure I had thought I would ever receive it, to know its weight."

"And how does it feel – how do *you* feel, now you have it?"

She crouched down beside it, as it lay on the bed, glistening and glittering, like an oily droplet, light still emanating from it. She studied it silently, hearing the ragged breathing from the cold and shadowed figure, awake to all the sensations of light battling against the dark, cold reaching out into the warmth. She shivered as the frosty tendrils staining the floor reached her, questing outwards from the figure. She inched away, still studying the glowing orb.

"I don't really feel any different. Is that strange? I will keep this though, as I will never get my own back. This will be a useful reminder, and may provide some solace."

She slid it back inside the stocking, and the light receded. She took a moment to glance at the gift tag, and a sad smile twisted her mouth. Her thumb stroked across the gilded lettering, then she squared her shoulders and clenched her jaw.

The visitor by the door faded away, taking the smell of time with them, leaving only the glitter of frost shimmering like tinsel, on the tree.

MISTLETOE

Janet Patrick

For centuries he stood witness
Sheltering fugitive, owl or king
In silent dignity,
Morning light his soft regalia.
She came to him in winter,
Radiant in green with lustrous pearls,
Swathing him in her braids
To heal the wounds of time.
Stranger she, yet deeply welcome
Her gift worn so lightly
Received with love
Unsought is harmony gained.

A TRUE CHRISTMAS STORY

John Nevinson

Christmas was going to be very different this year. For the first time in our lives, we were not all going to be together for the holiday---my sister's husband had just had a cataract operation and wasn't able to drive north to Carlisle, and Mum was becoming too frail to sally forth on the packed trains to Manchester. It would seem a sadly depleted table on Christmas Day so, as we were breaking with tradition, I decided Mum and I would have our first-ever Christmas dinner out. A table for two was reserved at a swish hotel in the Eden Valley and, as I'm not a driver, a taxi was booked to ferry us out and home again on Christmas Day.

I went over to my mother's bungalow after breakfast, and we had a leisurely Christmas morning. At midday, our usual friendly taxi driver arrived as prompt as he always was. Danny was the ideal man for the day---barrel-chested, florid-faced, white-bearded, twinkle-eyed and mischievously funny. He dropped us at the hotel door, and said he would be back about 2.30.

Mum and I were greeted in the entrance hall, and I placed our coats up on the tree-like coat rack, one of those upright wooden ones with several arms branching out. Already three or four coats were hanging there. I escorted Mum to the bar area for a drink, and within minutes we were taken to our table in the seasonally-decorated conservatory. Soon we were tucking in to a delicious Christmas dinner, served by friendly staff, and the fact that everything was so different from our usual family day was made easier by the novelty of the surroundings.

Just after two o'clock, full of turkey and Christmas pudding (and a little wine!) we went into the lounge, and eased ourselves dozily into the comfy chairs. It seemed we hadn't been there for five minutes when a girl came over and said, "Mr Nevinson? Your taxi is here." I thought there must be a mistake, but glancing through the windows, recognised our own Father Christmas.

I went to fetch the coats, and the tree-stand had turned into a forest. Each of the ten arms had three or four coats on, mostly black, hanging there like a colony of bats, and with great difficulty I extricated ours. Greeted effusively by Danny, we tottered over to the cab, and I climbed in, already feeling that I had eaten too much---so much so that I didn't want to button up the coat over a straining middle!

There was much banter with Danny before he dropped us at Mum's bungalow. We walked up the path, laughing that there was no washing-up to do—it was going to be such an easy afternoon this year. It was when I announced that I was feeling quite happily dozy and would go back to my house and have a lie-down that Mum said, "What's that on your coat?"

I looked down. It was the most beautiful large expensive silver brooch.

"You've got the wrong coat!" said Mum, quicker off the mark than me, who wondered why this mysterious brooch had attached itself to my smart new short black coat.

No chance of a post-prandial lie-down now!

"Sorry to bother you," I said, as the phone at the hotel was picked up.

"Yes?" replied a tinny voice on the telephone.

"I have just arrived home from Christmas dinner with you, and I'm afraid I've picked up the wrong coat!"

Gosh, it sounded so stupid. The voice went to fetch the deputy manager.

"Hello? This is Philip. You have the wrong coat, sir?"

"Yes," I said lamely.

"And I have a very upset lady here..." he began.

"I'm sorry," I interrupted, "but I came out by taxi, and it'll be impossible to book another one now on Christmas afternoon, so if you just give me the lady's name and telephone number then I'll sort things out with her, and try to get the coat returned."

There was the briefest pause and Philip said, "Don't worry. I'll be at your house in the next twenty minutes and pick up the coat."

I started to tell him that was more than kind, but the line went dead. Half an hour later, I had my coat returned, and the Brooch Lady would soon have hers back.

"Didn't you notice the different buttoning?" asked Mum, after singing the praises of the deputy manager.

"When I fell into that taxi, I felt too stuffed to think of fastening it," I explained. And so awake now that there was no thought of having a snooze!

The following Christmas it was easy to persuade my visiting sister and her husband that a Christmas dinner at that same hotel would be a good idea. No major shopping. No sorting out Brussels sprouts on Christmas Eve. No working out pounds and ounces and minutes for the turkey. No getting up at an unearthly hour to put the oven on. No letting the Christmas pudding dry out. No washing up. No days of plundering the bony carcase to create turkey salad, turkey risotto, turkey and chips, turkey soup...

We dutifully dressed up and travelled in their car down the Eden Valley. As we walked into the hotel, a passing waiter directed us to a hatch where an attractive young girl sat with an assortment of buff-coloured cloakroom tickets in front of her. She smiled as she looked up, and said, "If you can take a ticket, I will check in your coats."

"Oh, that's a new idea," I smiled.

She wrinkled her nose.

"Well, it's necessary---last year some stupid man walked off with the wrong coat!"

There was half a second's hush before I heard the laughter.

"It was him! It was him!"

Pointing at me, my brother-in-law was grinning from ear to ear, as were my sister and mother.

So now, if I go out for a meal with them, or anybody else who has been regaled with the infamous tale of the stolen coat, I can be sure that, as it is time to go home, some wit in the party will say, "Now just check carefully, John. Are you sure you've got the right coat? No nice silver brooch...?"

THE SPIRIT OF CHRISTMAS

Susan Cartwright-Smith

It was a beautiful scene – the warmth and twinkle of a family's window, dressed in its finery for Christmas. The bright light piercing against the growing gloom of a winter evening. Always a cosy yellow glow. Beckoning. Warm.

The smell of cinnamon and woodsmoke overlay the chill tang of the snowy street. Cloves, orange peel, a ham cooking – the olfactory promises of good things. I shivered against the outside cold as the internal fire began to be stoked. This was the kind of scene to make you believe in all the Christmas miracles.

I looked through the window, only half-feeling like it was an intrusion. I could see the comforting scene inside; a Christmas tree, draped any old how, festooned with a mish-mash of lovingly crafted children's decorations, and a more serious attempt at display with fragile baubles and wooden trinkets. The twinkle of lights on the tree, carefully positioned so every bauble gleamed with the reflected beam made my eyes prickle with the winking, twinkling starlit effect. My breath gusted out, like smoke.

I could see a child playing inside; unusual playmates for usual toys as some of the decorations became incorporated into games – camels and kings joining with tin soldiers. The fire glowed in the hearth, the child seemed unaffected by the proximity of the heat.

My hands were cold, holding the packet I had been to collect; streaky bacon from the butcher. Thick rind which would be chopped up for the birds, a rare sight nowadays. A herald of Christmas, preparations for the feast always included wrapping the small sausages in bacon, and other traditions like keeping the goose grease for cooking potatoes in, and locating the silver sixpence. These traditions handed down through time, keeping the past alive. Of such things are memories made.

Once more my breath billowed out like smoke, and I knew that time was slipping away. The image in front of me began to dematerialise like curling drifts of fog, and the reality of the present day setting reasserted itself. The smell of dampened embers became wet leaf mould, the smell of spices just on the edge of senses. A block of impersonal flats took the place of the family home, and what had been my world faded out as a memory. The fire that had raged through from an overlooked candle or a glowing coal had claimed my parents and brother as I collected the butcher's parcel. Nothing left to mark what had stood there but memories and old photographs that no-one looked at any more.

I shiver as a car passes through me. I too, am as insubstantial as smoke, curling away like a snuffed out candle. I had run blindly into the street, that night, and had not seen or heard the horses of the speeding fire engine.

Still, Christmas is a time to be with family is it not? And I have been visiting them for a hundred years now. Some traditions are to be kept alive.

RANDOM ACTS OF CHRISTMAS KINDNESS

Ella Atherton

The first time I saw him he was leaning against the cream sandstone wall of Barclay's Bank. You remember the one, it's on the corner of English Street and Bank Street. I passed it most days on my way to work. The man was huddled in a muddy brown sleeping bag on the damp pavement. He looked like something left behind by garbage collectors. Incongruous really, compared to the richness of the Christmas decorations already festooning the centre of town. Like the Christmas tree - sent over from Norway each year - commanding a majestic view of the square. While flashing blue lights that looked like fire-flies, danced up and down the winter branches of the young trees. Shoppers hustling and bustling in an out of the shops with great purpose. And plenty of money judging by their bulging bags-for-life. The man on the other hand, had only one purpose; to relieve the shoppers of their spare change.

I wouldn't normally look at beggars in the street but the sound of his dog whimpering caught my attention. The wet nose of a brindled k9 peeping from beneath the man's sleeping bag touched my heart. On impulse I asked the man if I could give the dog a chewy stick. He nodded his assent. I proffered one and the dog took it politely, not ravenously as I expected. I was glad, and glad that he looked well cared for. I began to warm to the man. Especially when I noticed his smile as his dog hid the chewy stick beneath the bed to eat later. Something my own dog would do. The man said, 'Thank you', in good English with an accent I couldn't place. Being a social worker by training and a nosey-parker by nature, I had no hesitation in asking him where he'd come from.

'Manchester,' he said.

I knew his wasn't a Manchester accent and I was keen to know more...

As I looked beyond his shabby appearance, his overgrown beard and down-filled jacket that was threatening to spit feathers at any moment, I couldn't help noticing the warmth in his brown eyes; so full of intelligence yet mixed with deep sadness.

From then on, whenever I was in town, I made sure I had a good supply of dog treats. Although the man was collecting change, I never gave him any. I didn't approve of begging and was afraid the money would go towards drugs or alcohol. Though I had to admit, he didn't look like a drug or alcohol user. I took sandwiches instead. Which he shared with his dog. So I started bringing little trays of dog food too and bottles of water for Kenneth (I know, a silly name for a dog but he was already named when Ahmad rescued him).

Little by little I got to know Ahmad's story. His family were killed in Aleppo, he escaped before he could be forced into the army and made the arduous journey to Turkey, before being smuggled into Europe. He spent nine months living rough in Calais until the camp was torn down by the *gendarmes*. Ahmad tried many times to get to England, eventually stowing away in a lorry from Bulgaria. He made his way to a southern English town where the local authority, inundated with refugees, gave him a one-way ticket to Glasgow.

Partly on impulse and partly because he thought there was a checkpoint at the border, Ahmad got off the train in Carlisle.

The local authority in Carlisle referred him to Middlesbrough; the nearest Asylum processing centre. Ahmad filed his application but wasn't entitled to benefits. He was reduced to begging in the streets, which he hated. In his country he taught International Law at Aleppo University until the university was targeted and many students and faculty members were killed.

Ahmad now wanted to study British and European Law so that he could help other asylum seekers.

I put my social work hat on and referred him to the local food bank and suggested he volunteer for the Salvation Army or the Red Cross or both. This would help build community relationships and might even prove to the authorities that he could be a valuable member of society. I also introduced him to a friend at the Citizen's Advice Bureau, a lawyer in her own right, who would help and support Ahmad. I felt sure that his good English would stand him in good stead.

I missed Ahmad during weeks leading up to Christmas. His pitch was taken by someone else. Not surprising really, it was a lucrative spot between two banks and a thriving shopping centre.

Two days before Christmas I saw Kenneth trotting alone in the centre of town; his lead trailing behind him.

'Kenneth, Kenneth,' I called. 'Here, boy.'

Kenneth recognised me immediately, wagged his tail furiously and snuffled my pocket for his usual treats. I bent down to fluff his ears.

'Where's Ahmad, Kenneth? What happened to him?'

'Here I am,' came a voice.

I looked up and there was Ahmad. The same warm brown eyes, but his beard was neatly trimmed and he was wearing a smart business suit, a dark knee-length coat and highly-polished, leather shoes.

'Wow,' I said, leaping to my feet. 'You shall go to the ball!'

Before I could stop myself, I gave Ahmad a big hug, which he returned twofold.

'Come. Coffee,' he laughed, taking my hand and guiding me to a nearby coffee shop. He tied Kenneth to a bike stand, making sure the knot was tight, 'Good boy,' said Ahmad. 'Stay.'

We sat in a window seat to keep an eye on Kenneth, and Ahmad ordered a latte for me and an Espresso for himself. He told me he had taken my advice and my friend at CAB referred him to the Home Office, where his application for asylum was fast-tracked. It was clear from his references from The Salvation Army and British Red Cross, that Ahmad was committed to life in England. His new contacts had also secured him an internship at the solicitor's on Castle Street. He'd even won a bursary to read British and European Law at Cumbria University.

Ahmad leaned across the table and gently took my hand in his.

'I could not have done it without you,' he said. 'You showed me kindness where others passed by. You were the Good Samaritan in your Christian Bible, you were the one who gave shelter to Mary and Joseph...'

'Okay, Ahmad, I get it.' My laughter interrupted his flow.

Ahmad laughed too, but continued... 'As a good Muslim in your country I wish to celebrate your Christmas. You and your chaperone must come to my new apartment. I will make you good Arabic food. I will be honoured if you say yes.'

'Yes, yes,' I said, 'I'd love to come.'

As I contemplated who my 'chaperone' might be, I decided it was the ideal job for my dog, Toby. I knew he'd get on well with Kenneth and it meant we could all be together at Christmas... and who knows? This could be the start of many happy Christmases together...

Made in the USA
Columbia, SC
15 November 2018